# A Place for Nicholas

# A Place for Nicholas

Lucy Floyd

Illustrated by David McPhail

**Green Light Readers**
**Harcourt, Inc.**
Orlando Austin New York San Diego Toronto London

Nicholas wanted a place.
Not just any place.
He wanted his own place.

"You have this house," said Dad.
"But everybody is here," said Nicholas.

"You have this yard," said Kelly.
"But everybody is here," said Nicholas.

"You have this room," said Mom.
"But Jeff is here," said Nicholas.

"I'll make a place for you," said Jeff.
"But you are too little," said Nicholas.

"Come back soon," said Jeff. "You'll see."

Nicholas did see.
And now he has his very own place!

# How Did That Happen?

Jeff turned Nicholas's room into a new special place. Did you ever turn something old into something new? Now you can!

# WHAT YOU'LL NEED

Scissors, markers, glue, tape—
and lots of old stuff!

hoose things you can use
make something new.

Show a friend what you made.
Tell what you started with and
how you changed it.

# Places to Play

Nicholas likes to play in his
very own special place.
Where do you like to play?

## WHAT YOU'LL NEED

paper

crayons or markers

**1** Fold a piece of paper in half. Write INSIDE and OUTSIDE at the top.

**2** Make a list of all the games and activities you like to do inside and outside.

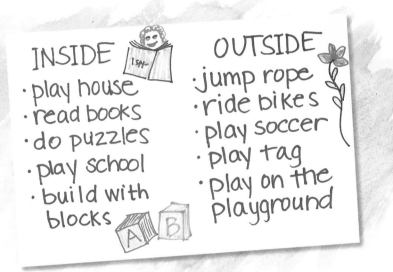

INSIDE
- play house
- read books
- do puzzles
- play school
- build with blocks

OUTSIDE
- jump rope
- ride bikes
- play soccer
- play tag
- play on the playground

**3** Share your ideas with a friend. Then go and play—inside and outside!

# Meet the Author and Illustrator

*Lucy Floyd*

*David McPhail*

Lucy Floyd's special place when she was growing up was her grandparents' farm, where her grandmother would tell her stories. David McPhail's special place was the woods near his house, where he could watch animals play. They both hope you can find your very own special place, too!

Requests for permission to make copies of any part of the work should be mailed to
the following address: Permissions Department, Harcourt, Inc., 6277 Sea Harbor
Drive, Orlando, Florida 32887-6777.

www.HarcourtBooks.com

First Green Light Readers edition 2005
*Green Light Readers* is a trademark of Harcourt, Inc., registered in the United States
of America and/or other jurisdictions.

Library of Congress Cataloging-in-Publication Data
Floyd, Lucy.
A place for Nicholas/Lucy Floyd; illustrated by David McPhail.
p.  cm.
"Green Light Readers."
Summary: Nicholas wants a place that is his very own, and his younger brother
finds a way to help.
[1. Solitude—Fiction.  2. Brothers—Fiction.  3. Family life—Fiction.]
I. McPhail, David, 1940– ill.  II. Title.  III. Series: Green Light reader.
PZ7.F6698Pl  2005
[E]—dc22    2003026725
ISBN 0-15-205150-3
ISBN 0-15-205149-X pb

A C E G H F D B
A C E G H F D B (pb)

**Ages 5–7**
**Grades:  1**
**Guided Reading Level: F**
**Reading Recovery Level: 9–10**

## Green Light Readers
### For the reader who's ready to GO!

"A must-have for any family with a beginning reader."—*Boston Sunday Herald*

"You can't go wrong with adding several copies of these terrific books to your beginning-to-read collection."—*School Library Journal*

"A winner for the beginner."—*Booklist*

## Five Tips to Help Your Child Become a Great Reader

**1.** Get involved. Reading aloud to and with your child is just as important as encouraging your child to read independently.

**2.** Be curious. Ask questions about what your child is reading.

**3.** Make reading fun. Allow your child to pick books on subjects that interest her or him.

**4.** Words are everywhere—not just in books. Practice reading signs, packages, and cereal boxes with your child.

**5.** Set a good example. Make sure your child sees YOU reading.

## Why Green Light Readers Is the Best Series for Your New Reader

- Created exclusively for beginning readers by some of the biggest and brightest names in children's books

- Reinforces the reading skills your child is learning in school

- Encourages children to read—and finish—books by themselves

- Offers extra enrichment through fun, age-appropriate activities unique to each story

- Incorporates characteristics of the Reading Recovery program used by educators

- Developed with Harcourt School Publishers and credentialed educational consultants